W9-CIO-689

Montgomery, R
Mo   A
      Indian trail

DATE DUE			

BIRCH GROVE
Hazel Widlund Media Center
Independent School District No. 279
Osseo, Minnesota
Osseo Area Schools, I.S.D. 279
Maple Grove, MN   55369

"I DON'T LIKE CHOOSE YOUR OWN ADVENTURE® BOOKS, I *LOVE* THEM!" says Jessica Gordon, age 10. And now, kids between the ages of six and nine can choose their own adventure, too. Here's what kids have to say about the Skylark Choose Your Own Adventure® books.

"These are my favorite books because you can pick whatever choice you want—and the story is all about you."
—Katy Alson, *age 8*

"I love finding out how my story will end."
—Joss Williams, *age 9*

"I like all the illustrations!"
—Savitri Brightfield, *age 7*

"A six-year-old friend and I have lots of fun making the decisions together."
—Peggy Marcus *(adult)*

Bantam Skylark Books in the Choose Your Own
  Adventure® Series
Ask your bookseller for the books you have missed

INDIAN TRAIL

R. A. MONTGOMERY

ILLUSTRATED BY LESLIE MORRILL

BIRCH GROVE
Hazel Widlund Media Center
Independent School District No. 279
Osseo, Minnesota

A BANTAM SKYLARK BOOK®
TORONTO · NEW YORK · LONDON · SYDNEY

RL 2, 007-009

INDIAN TRAIL
A Bantam Skylark Book / April 1983

CHOOSE YOUR OWN ADVENTURE® is a registered
trademark of Bantam Books, Inc.
Original Conception of Edward Packard

Skylark Books is a registered trademark of
Bantam Books, Inc.
Registered in U.S. Patent and Trademark Office
and elsewhere.

All rights reserved.
Copyright © 1983 by Raymond A. Montgomery, Jr.
Cover art and inside illustrations copyright © 1983 by
Bantam Books, Inc.
This book may not be reproduced in whole or in part, by
mimeograph or any other means, without permission.
For information address: Bantam Books, Inc.

ISBN 0-553-15201-7

Published simultaneously in the United States and Canada

Bantam Books are published by Bantam Books, Inc. Its trademark, consisting of the words "Bantam Books" and the por-
trayal of a rooster, is Registered in U.S. Patent and Trademark
Office and in other countries. Marca Registrada. Bantam
Books, Inc., 666 Fifth Avenue, New York, New York 10103.

PRINTED IN THE UNITED STATES OF AMERICA

CW   0 9 8 7 6 5 4 3 2 1

To Anson & Ramsey
With special thanks
to Julius Goodman
for his editorial expertise

READ THIS FIRST!!!

Most books are about other people.
This book is about you!
What happens to you depends on what you decide to do.
Do not read this book from the first page through to the last page. Instead, start on page one and read until you come to your first choice. Then turn to the page shown and see what happens.
When you come to the end of a story, go back and start a new adventure.
Be careful! There are wolves and bears in the hills. There are also enemy Indian tribes.
Good luck on your journey!

You are standing outside your pueblo village. It is early morning, before dawn. Everyone else in your village is still sleeping.

It hasn't rained for weeks. The streams have dried up, and the crops of corn, beans, and squash lie brown and withered in the fields. If rain doesn't come soon, the crops will die, and your people will have no food.

Your father has told you about Indian spirits called kachinas, who inhabit the earth and the skies. Your whole village has prayed to the kachinas with dances and secret ceremonies held in kivas, special underground rooms of the pueblo.

You want the kachinas to ask the gods of rain and crops to help your village. Your father has told you that in the past sometimes the kachinas brought rain and the crops were saved. Sometimes they didn't help and your people died.

Turn to page 2.

2 You want to help your people. You want to help bring rain. You have danced in the kachina dances, but still it has not rained.

You talk the problem over with your friend, Running Foot. Together you decide to search for the kachinas. You will ask them to bring rain to the crops. The trail to their dwelling place is long and hard. Some of the older villagers say it is dangerous, but you will go anyway.

It is time to go get Running Foot and begin your journey before the village awakens.

Turn to page 5.

As you set out to get Running Foot, Wise **5** One, your grandfather, comes out of his pueblo. "It is good to go in search of the kachinas," he tells you. "You are very brave." How did he know where you were going?

Wise One looks up to the sky, which is beginning to show morning colors. "When I was young," he says, "I wanted to go to the home of the kachinas, but I was not brave enough." Wise One smiles at you. "I would like to go now. Will you let me come with you?"

You want to go alone with Running Foot, but it might be disrespectful not to take grandfather. What should you do?

If you say, "Running Foot and I planned to search by ourselves. I will take you with me in my heart," go on to page 6.

If you say, "I will get Running Foot. Then we will all leave together," turn to page 9.

6   You bid farewell to your grandfather. You find Running Foot in his bedroll. "Wake up," you whisper. "Time to find the kachinas."

Together you hurry away from the pueblo, carrying your small bundles of food and jars of water. You cross the dried-up stream, and head through the hills toward the high mountains. You grow hot and thirsty as you cross the dry, baked ground.

You come to a trail that winds through the hills. "This must be the trail to the kachinas," Running Foot says. The trail is steep. It curves and twists. You round a bend and stop suddenly. In front of you stands a large, gray wolf. He is licking his lips over a fallen deer. When he sees you he snarls, showing his huge yellow teeth.

If you try to scare the wolf away, turn to page 12.

If you decide to leave the wolf alone and find a new trail, turn to page 14.

You hurry to wake Running Foot. As you walk back across the courtyard, you tell him that Wise One is coming, too. Running Foot is disappointed at first. Then he says, "Perhaps your grandfather will be helpful. He knows more than we do. It will be good to have him along."

In the courtyard you see three dogs. One of them is named Great Eye. He wags his tail and runs to meet you.

Great Eye is a good friend. You like to think of him as your very own dog, even though he belongs to the whole village. You and Great Eye have been on many adventures before. You decide to take him along, too.

When you get to grandfather's house, he is standing outside, waiting. He is holding a small bundle. You want to ask him what is in the bundle, but perhaps it is a secret.

If you ask Wise One about the bundle, turn to page 17.

If you wait for Wise One to tell you about the bundle, go on to page 10.

10   You respect Wise One. He will tell you about the bundle in good time. You put the bundle out of your mind and start walking up the mountain trail.

Wise One walks slowly. You and Running Foot walk with him. Great Eye races ahead and then returns, and then races ahead again.

Night comes, and it is time to rest. You and

Running Foot make a fire. In the distance
you hear the cry of a mountain lion and the
howl of a wolf. The stars shine. It is cold.
Even the fire does not warm you.

Grandfather sits quietly. Great Eye curls up
at his feet.

You cannot sleep. You stare into the darkness.

Turn to page 26.

12   You hope that you can scare the wolf away with your short, sharp spear. You hurl the spear at the wolf. Running Foot stands by your side, ready with his spear.

Your spear hits the wolf in the side, near a hind leg. The wolf snarls in pain and anger. It runs off, yelping.

You are worried. You had meant only to scare off the wolf, not to hurt it.

"Running Foot, what should we do? We can't let the wolf die in pain. We must find it."

"No," says Running Foot. "We came to search for the kachinas, not to hunt the wolf."

If you decide you must follow the wolf, turn to page 24.

If you listen to Running Foot and continue to look for the kachinas, turn to page 31.

You decide to leave the wolf alone. Running Foot backs slowly away. The wolf snarls again. You know you are safe if you don't get too close. You follow Running Foot and leave the wolf to its meal.

You find a new trail and climb high into the mountains. The rocks, the animals, the trees seem new and strange. It is like a different world. You feel very far from home.

The hours slip by and you forget the time. You come to a narrow ridge that separates two mountains. The trail runs across loose, slippery rocks.

Running Foot cautiously starts across the ridge, careful not to disturb the loose rocks. Then he slips.

The rocks underneath him give way and he tumbles. He gets up slowly, unhurt. The rocks stop sliding, but at any moment they could slide again.

If you decide to try to cross the ridge, turn to page 28.

If you turn back and try to find a new route, turn to page 23.

"Wise One," you ask, "what is in the bundle?"

He hands it to you and says, "See for yourself." You unwrap the bundle and find a red, white, and yellow wooden doll.

It is a kachina doll! And it is alive!

The doll jumps to the ground. You, Running Foot, Great Eye, and Wise One stare at the doll as it grows before your eyes.

It moves slowly at first. Then, moving faster and faster, it races up the hill.

"Wise One, where is it going?"

"Let us follow it."

Turn to page 20.

You and Running Foot walk away from the bear.

The bear follows you with its eyes. Its eyes are clouded with pain, and you feel ashamed. But when you turn back, the bear is gone, and in its place stands a kachina.

"If you want our help, then you must help others." The kachina is angry. In a flash he vanishes. You and Running Foot are left alone.

The End

20   You, Running Foot, Wise One, and Great Eye follow the kachina doll, which is now far ahead.

"Grandfather, where did the kachina come from? Why did you have it?"

"The doll is the spirit of the kachinas," Wise One explains. "The kachinas are spirits of the trees, the water, the land, the birds, and the sky. If we follow the doll, it will lead us to the kachinas. Then the rains will come. Hurry now. We have far to go."

The End

You turn back. The kachinas could be anywhere. You decide it would be foolish to risk injury or death in the mountains.

You and Running Foot start down into a canyon. The path is steep and rocky.

Wait! You hear a strange sound. Quietly, the two of you peek over a boulder into the canyon. A group of men are tying up their horses and silently leaving on foot down a small path.

They are Apaches! The Apaches are enemies of your tribe. They sometimes raid your village and steal the food. This is a war party.

If you leave immediately to warn your village, turn to page 38.

If you decide to follow the Apaches to learn their plan, turn to page 44.

24 The elders have taught you to respect all living things. The wolf should not be left to die slowly of its wound. Bright red drops of blood dot the ground. You tell Running Foot you must try to find the wolf. Running Foot finally agrees.

"Running Foot, go to the left. I'll follow the trail of blood. Be careful."

It is dangerous to follow the wolf. Your

steps are slow and careful. Quietly and cautiously you creep along. You follow the trail of blood down a slope and into a canyon.

"Help! Help!"

You freeze in your tracks. Has the wolf caught Running Foot? The sound of his voice comes from the canyon.

You creep around three enormous boulders. Your sharp skinning knife is in your hand.

You carefully rise up tall and look over the boulders.

Turn to page 32.

At last dawn comes. You see the sun on the mountaintops. You listen to the birds. You hear the stream running through the valley. You feel the spirit of the land. You feel kachinas all around you.

You stand up and spread your arms to the sky.

"O great kachinas, my people need your help. O kachinas, please come down to our village. Bring rain to our gardens. Bring life to our people."

Wise One nods his approval. "They will come. Have no fear." He opens his bundle and takes out an offering of corn and beans, which he places on a rock.

You listen and wait. You see no kachinas.

But you see that in the valley clouds are beginning to gather. You hear the roll of thunder. The rains will come.

The End

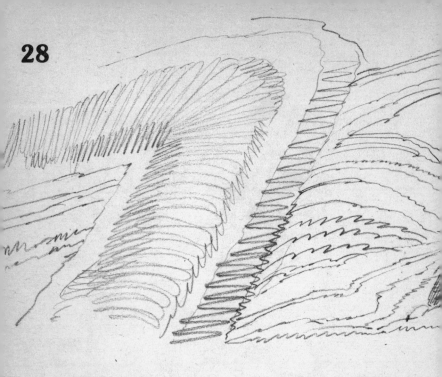

It's dangerous, but you want to try to cross the ridge. Running Foot is nervous and so are you. You walk carefully. Slowly, you make your way across the loose rocks. Then your foot hits a stone and sends it rolling down the mountainside, deep into the canyon below. You stop and listen. Have you started a landslide? You hold your breath. Running Foot stands shaking beside you. He listens, too.

The rocks are steady. You are safe!

Running Foot races ahead. You see him

jump around the patches of snow that remain in the crags and high valleys.

You are very tired. You feel dizzy and sick to your stomach. You see small black dots in front of your eyes. You feel cold, even in the sun.

If you run to catch up with Running Foot, turn to page 35.

If you decide to sit down and rest, turn to page 36.

Running Foot is right. You must continue your journey. You hope the wolf wasn't badly hurt.

As you walk along the trail, you see a black crow circling above you. It swoops down and caws, "Follow me."

The crow flies in front of you, so close you could touch it. It leads you along many winding trails. You and Running Foot follow, in and out between the rocky cliffs, until suddenly the crow is gone!

Poof! It has vanished from the sky. You are high in the mountains, far from the pueblo. There is no path.

Turn to page 41.

32 You see Running Foot lying on the ground. The wolf stands over him, about to attack.

With a rush you lunge at the wolf with your knife.

Then it happens! The wolf changes into a kachina! He is tall and broad shouldered, and his head is crowned with bright feathers. He speaks.

"So, you have found us, little ones. You are very brave, but you need not kill.

"Remember, all living things have the right to their lives. Go now. Return to your village. Rain will come."

Large, gray clouds fill the sky. As you turn back to your village, the first drops of rain touch your arms and head. The crops will live; your people will have food. You and Running Foot have brought the kachinas back.

The End

You try to catch up with Running Foot. **35** Soon you reach a small stream, and you stop to drink some of the cool, clear water. You feel a little better, but you are too tired to go on. You hope Running Foot will return.

You fall asleep. When you awaken, Running Foot is at your side. "Here, chew this bark," he says. "It will make you feel better and we can . . ."

Suddenly, Running Foot stops talking. You turn. A bear is standing not far from you.

There is an arrow sticking out of the bear's side. He seems helpless. He looks at you with fear, too weak to attack. You want to help, but Running Foot wants to leave quickly.

*If you decide to help the bear,
turn to page 42.*

If you leave the bear, turn to page 18.

36 You feel too sick to catch up with Running Foot. Using a flint and stone you build a small fire. Where is Running Foot?

As you sit by the fire, a figure comes out from behind a clump of bushes. It is a kachina, wearing a headdress of large, bright feathers. He stands tall and straight.

"You are sick, my friend. I will help you."

The kachina chants a healing song. You grow warm and cozy, and soon you feel the sickness leave your body. You are well again. You sleep, and when you awaken, Running Foot is asleep at your side. It is a new day. You eat corn for breakfast. You tell Running Foot about the kachina.

You and Running Foot climb high into the mountains. You can see across the valley to distant peaks. You see the desert far below you. You can even see your village.

Turn to page 46.

You and Running Foot must warn your people about the Apaches! You run like the deer. You almost fall, but you don't. You keep on running.

One of the Apaches spies you. He shouts a warning to the others, and they give chase. Your heart pounds loudly in your chest as you run for your life.

Turn to page 50.

Running Foot suggests that you light a fire and pray to the kachinas. "Perhaps they will hear us better, high up in the mountains. Maybe that is why the crow brought us here."

You gather a large pile of dry branches and pine cones. Then Running Foot takes a flint from his leather pouch and strikes it on a stone. The pine cones catch the spark, and a tiny flame appears.

The flame grows tall, and the heat of the fire drives you back. Shadows dance, for now it is night.

Then, boom! Crash! Thunder roars through the mountains. Lightning rips open the sky.

Before you have a chance to offer up your prayer, the kachinas are around you.

A huge kachina rises beyond the ring of fire. He does not speak, but in his hands he holds raindrops. The crops will live.

You did it! You and Running Foot have found the kachinas.

The End

42 You feel you must help the bear. You watch to make sure that the bear is too weak to hurt you. Then Running Foot goes to the bear and carefully removes the arrow. He brings water, washes the wound, and lets the bear drink.

Suddenly you hear a voice. You turn and see three kachinas. One speaks.

"You are brave and you are kind. You have helped the bear, and now we will help your people. The rains will come."

You and Running Foot return happily to your village.

The End

"Let us follow the Apaches," you tell Running Foot.

You keep low and stay out of sight. You are quiet and don't let them spot you.

Later in the day the Apaches stop and make camp. You and Running Foot creep forward and listen to what they are saying. The leader says, "We will attack the pueblo village at dawn. They will never expect us to come on foot. We will take everything we need."

Turn to page 48.

Higher and higher you climb. The trail gets steeper and rockier. You have to shade your eyes from the bright, hot sun.

You find no more kachinas. Running Foot is as disappointed as you are.

"We have not found any kachinas to bring rain, but a kachina found me when I was sick," you say. "Let us go back to the pueblo. I am sure the kachinas will come there to help just as one came to help me."

"And think of the story we have to tell," says Running Foot with a laugh.

Together you start toward home.

The End

You and Running Foot tiptoe away from the Apache camp. You are careful not to make any noise. You feel like running. You want to be far from these fierce warriors. Yet you force yourself to walk slowly, with silent footsteps. You know you must leave no trail for the warriors to follow. Your legs ache from being so careful. Your journey home seems to take forever. Near dawn, you and Running Foot reach the stream by your pueblo.

Now you run! You dash into your village,
yelling, "Raid! Apache raid!"

Three men in the courtyard hear you.
They pick up their weapons. Others hear
your shouts, and they come running, too.

You have saved your village. You and
Running Foot are heroes.

The End

You and Running Foot race down the trail and leap over the rocks.

The Apaches are fast, but you are faster. Your breath comes in gasps. Running Foot pants loudly beside you.

It seems like hours before you come to the fields outside the village. You shout with all your might. "Apaches! Apaches!"

Your people run to meet you. The Apaches are turned away with a shower of arrows and spears. They scatter into the hills.

Good for you! You saved the village from attack. Maybe that was the gift of the kachinas. Maybe now the kachinas will send rain for the crops. You feel sure that they will.

The End

ABOUT THE AUTHOR

R. A. Montgomery is an educator and publisher. A graduate of Williams College, he also studied in graduate programs at Yale University and New York University. After serving in a variety of administrative capacities at Williston Academy and Columbia University, he co-founded the Waitsfield Summer School in 1965. Following that, Montgomery helped found a research and development firm specializing in the development of educational programs. He worked for several years as a consultant to the Peace Corps in Washington, D.C. and West Africa. For the last seven years, he has been both a writer and a publisher.

ABOUT THE ILLUSTRATOR

Leslie Morrill is a designer and illustrator whose work has won him numerous awards. He has illustrated over thirty books for children, including the Bantam Classic edition of *The Wind in the Willows*. His work has also appeared frequently in *Cricket* magazine. A graduate of the Boston Museum School of Fine Arts, Mr. Morrill lives near Boston, Massachusetts.

WANT TO READ THE MOST EXCITING BOOKS AROUND?
CHOOSE CHOOSE YOUR OWN ADVENTURE®

Everybody loves CHOOSE YOUR OWN ADVENTURE® books because the stories are about *you*. Each book is loaded with choices that only *you* can make. Instead of reading from the first page to the last page, you read until you come to your first choice. Then, depending on your decision, you turn to a new page to see what happens next. And you can keep reading and rereading CHOOSE YOUR OWN ADVENTURE® books because every choice leads to a new adventure and there are lots of different ways for the story to end.

Buy these great CHOOSE YOUR OWN ADVENTURE® books, available wherever Bantam Skylark books are sold or use the handy coupon below for ordering:

☐ THE HAUNTED HOUSE by R. A. Montgomery (15119-3 * $1.75)
☐ THE CIRCUS by Edward Packard (15120-7 * $1.75)
☐ SUNKEN TREASURE by Edward Packard (15150-9 * $1.75)
☐ SUNKEN TREASURE (Hardcover * 05018-4 * $6.95/$7.95 in Canada)
☐ YOUR VERY OWN ROBOT by R. A. Montgomery (15149-5 * $1.75)
☐ YOUR VERY OWN ROBOT
   (Hardcover * 05019-2 * $6.95/$7.95 in Canada)
☐ GORGA, THE SPACE MONSTER by Edward Packard
   (15161-4 * $1.75)
☐ GORGA, THE SPACE MONSTER
   (Hardcover * 05031-1 * $6.95/$7.95 in Canada)
☐ THE GREEN SLIME by R. A. Montgomery (15162-2 * $1.75)
☐ THE GREEN SLIME (Hardcover * 05032-X * $6.95/$7.95 in Canada)
☐ HELP! YOU'RE SHRINKING by Edward Packard (15195-9 * $1.95)
☒ INDIAN TRAIL by R. A. Montgomery (15201-7 * $1.95)

Bantam Books, Inc., Dept. AV5, 414 East Golf Road, Des Plaines, Ill. 60016

Please send me the books I have checked above. I am enclosing $1,000,0000,00,000
(please add $1.25 to cover postage and handling, send check or money order—
no cash or C.O.D.'s please).

Mr/Ms _____

Address _____

City/State _____ Zip _____
                                            AV8—4/83
Please allow four to six weeks for delivery. This offer expires 10/83.

DO YOU LOVE
CHOOSE YOUR OWN ADVENTURE®?
Let your older brothers and sisters in on the fun.

You know how great CHOOSE YOUR OWN AD-VENTURE® books are to read over and over again. But did you know that there are CHOOSE YOUR OWN ADVENTURE® books for older kids too? They're just as much fun as the CHOOSE YOUR OWN AD-VENTURE® books you read and they're filled with the same kinds of decisions—but they're longer and have even more ways for the story to end.

So get your older brothers and sisters and anyone else you know between the ages of nine and thirteen in on the fun by introducing them to the exciting world of CHOOSE YOUR OWN ADVENTURE®.

There are over twenty CHOOSE YOUR OWN AD-VENTURE® books for older kids now available wherever Bantam paperbacks are sold.

AV9—4/83

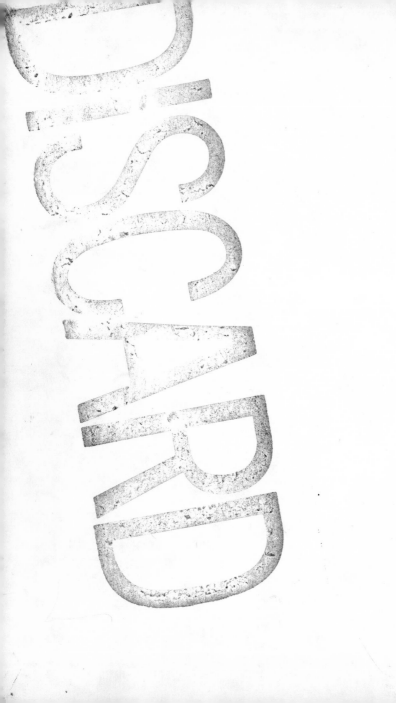